SNOWFLAKE DREAMS

A MOUNTAIN TALE

Written by Kristen Halverson

Illustrated by Masha Somova

For the Basalt Library.

Enjoy this mountain story!

Kristin Halverson

2019

ISBN: 978-1729562543 (Paperback)
ISBN: 978-1684549986 (Hardcover)

Any references to historical events, real people, or real places are used fictitiously. Names, characters, and places are products of the author's imagination.

Front cover design by Masha Somova
Interior Illustration designs by Masha Somova

Book Layout by Indie Publishing Group

Photo of Maroon Bells by Kan Khampanya, 123RF

First printing, 2018

Kristen Halverson, Publisher
14104 225th Street
Elkader, Iowa

www.kristenhalverson.com

For Kendall and Douglas Knaus,

This book honors their love for Aspen, winter sports, and the Rocky Mountains.

In addition, this storybook honors the

Aspen Snowmass Give A Flake Campaign

as a portion of book proceeds benefit Protect Our Winters.

Once upon a time, there lived a very curious and kind bear named Sasha, who dreamed about learning how to downhill ski. Sasha loved nature and wanted the best for his fellow animal friends who lived in the mountains. Sasha grew up in a faraway place called Snowflake Village.

His best friend Pasha was a very wise bear, who lived in a log cabin on top of the mountain.

He always shared his warm smile with everyone. Pasha had spent his life teaching skiing. Most of all, Pasha was a very patient teacher, and enjoyed sharing tales of the mountain from long ago with his students.

Snowflake Mountain
-Ski School-

It was a perfect day to travel to Pasha's home because of the great weather. Pasha greeted Sasha with a big smile. Sasha said, "I need your help because I finally want to learn how to downhill ski. I am also very curious about our mountains." Pasha replied, "I would love to teach you how to ski. Why do you want to learn now? You have always sat up beneath the trees and watched everyone." Sasha answered, "My mom gave me skis for my birthday. I have been reading books about downhill skiing too. It looks like so much fun! I want to feel the wind in my face!"

Pasha was thrilled to hear this news. Pasha said, "I will be happy to teach you. I think it's great that you have been reading about skiing. Sasha, go home and get some sleep. We will start your lesson early in the morning. I will also teach you how to take care of our mountains." Sasha cheered, "Great! I will see you in the morning!"

As Sasha hiked through the snow covered aspen trees toward his cabin, he felt the snow beginning to fall upon his thick fur. Suddenly, he saw the most colorful and magical looking snowflakes. They were dancing and bouncing in the wind. He noticed one snowflake that glowed. Then he tried to catch it with his big paws.

The dancing snowflake made a ringing noise which sounded like a bell. It whispered, "Sasha, make your dearest wish." In an instant, the snowflake blew away in the wind.

A moment after he made his wish, Sasha heard a peaceful sound coming from the trees swaying in the wind. As he looked up to admire them, the leaves turned yellow. Although it was winter, the bright aspen leaves surrounded him. Sasha thought to himself, "This must be a dream!"

When Sasha returned home, he went to bed dreaming about his ski lesson the next day along with the magical snowflake. Morning arrived, and Sasha was excited about his first downhill ski lesson.

As he munched on breakfast biscuits, Sasha heard Pasha calling his name. Sasha quickly grabbed his ski gear and headed outside to greet him. Sasha hollered, "I am ready for an awesome day!" Pasha shouted, "Great! Let's go have some fun!"

Sasha and Pasha put their skis in a sleigh. They let their horse friend, Tempo take them to the ski school. Pasha nudged Tempo and said, "I know a secret path to get us there quickly. Take the trail that has the incredible mountain views. It is so beautiful! We might see some deer and moose too!"

When they arrived, Pasha said, "First, I will share some important safety lessons. Then, I will have you learn without poles. Sasha, you can follow me as I ski down the tiny bear hill. We will add your poles later." Pasha spent the entire morning showing Sasha how to slide and stop on his thin skis. Sasha cheered, "Wow, I am really skiing! It is so much fun! I can't wait to ski down Snowflake Mountain!"

They took a break for lunch and went to the Bear Honey Cafe at the top of the mountain. Sasha wondered if he should tell Pasha about the magical snowflake. He did not want Pasha to laugh at him. As they ate their chocolate chip cookies and sipped on hot chocolate, Pasha shared how to take care of nature and the mountains.

Pasha said, "It takes a team effort to care for our rivers, trees, and mountains. There are some simple ways to help every day. For example, you can ride your alpine bear bicycles to the ski village, clean up your honey sandwich wrappers from outside your home, and return your mountain water bottles to the local bear recycle shop." Sasha smiled and said, "I know I can do these things!"

After they finished their delicious snacks, Sasha whispered, "Pasha, I need to share a story with you. Last night, I met a talking snowflake. I know it sounds funny! It asked me to make a wish close to my heart!"

Pasha replied, "I don't think it's funny. This mountain is a magical place for everyone. We all need to believe! Well, what did you wish for?"

Sasha answered, "I wished that there would always be snow on our mountains, enough fish to eat, and our rivers would be full of fresh water. I also wished to ski forever." Pasha roared, "We must all keep believing in our snowflake dreams! We are one big family living on this mountain together!"

Sasha told Pasha that he wanted to share his wish others. He said, "I have this t-shirt with Snowflake Mountain on it. I could add "Make a Difference" to the back to help create awareness with other bears and animals around the village on how to take care of the mountain."

Pasha was overjoyed to hear this news. He said, "I am so proud of you! I knew you were a very special bear. Now, let's get back to your ski lesson, and practice how to use your poles this afternoon. I want you to take the ski lift to the top of the mountain and ski down it tomorrow morning." Pasha spent the rest of the day showing Sasha how to use his poles and make turns.

SKI SCHOOL

The next day, they set out to ski down the mountain together. As they rode the ski lift, Pasha pointed toward all the different kinds of trees along trail.

Pasha said, "These trees are important for us as well. We must also do our part to protect them." When they reached the top of the mountain, Sasha shouted, "We made it! I can see the next village from up here. This is a dream come true! Pasha, you are the best teacher in the world!"

Sasha and Pasha lifted up their ski goggles and took one last look at the amazing mountain top views before they headed toward the beginner trail. Suddenly, the magical snowflake appeared.

It whispered, "Snowflake dreams are real! May there always be snow on the mountains for skiing, fish in our lakes, and rivers with clean water!" Sasha told the snowflake, "That was my wish!"

The snowflake replied, "Snowflake Mountain is a magical and special place."

In an instant the glowing snowflake blew away in the wind. Sasha and Pasha both smiled and cheered," Let's respect our mountain and give it our best every day!" Then, Pasha and Sasha took off down the ski slope and roared, "Long live Snowflake Mountain!"

Acknowledgement

I want to acknowledge the Aspen Daily News their September article of 2018 about the Aspen Snowmass Give A Flake Campaign. This inspiring article escalated my passion to join the movement to help protect the winters. In addition, it motivated my creative efforts to develop this heartfelt mountain and winter themed storybook.

Lastly, I want to extend my gratitude to my dedicated editorial team. Lisa Leuck, Alex Brown, and Ted G. Fleener demonstrated a steadfast commitment to this project. I am grateful for their wonderful support and excellent guidance. Lastly, I want to thank Masha Somova and Chrissy Hobbs for their talent and dedication.

CPSIA information can be obtained
at www.ICGtesting.com
Printed in the USA
BVHW021326171218
535789BV00008B/163/P